Bumpus Jumpus
Dinosaurumpus!

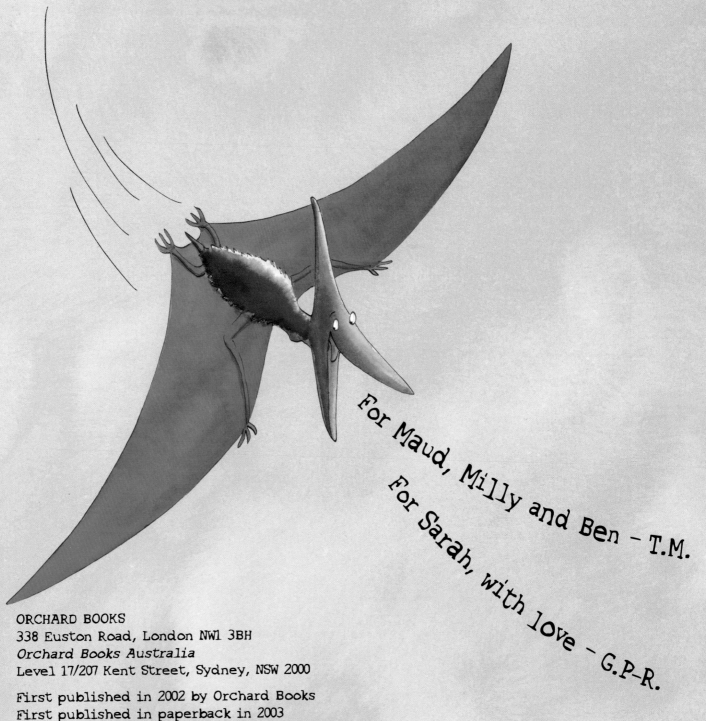

For Maud, Milly and Ben – T.M.
For Sarah, with love – G.P-R.

ORCHARD BOOKS
338 Euston Road, London NW1 3BH
Orchard Books Australia
Level 17/207 Kent Street, Sydney, NSW 2000

First published in 2002 by Orchard Books
First published in paperback in 2003
This edition published for Bookstart in 2006

ISBN 978 1 84616 373 9

Text © Tony Mitton 2002
Illustrations © Guy Parker-Rees 2002

A CIP catalogue record for this book is available from the British Library.

10 9 8 7 6 5 4 3 2

Printed in China

Orchard Books is a division of Hachette Children's Books,
an Hachette UK company. www.hachette.co.uk

Bumpus Jumpus Dinosaurumpus!

Tony Mitton

Guy Parker-Rees

ORCHARD BOOKS

There's a quake and a quiver
and a rumbling around.

It makes you shiver.
It's a thundery sound.

"Shake, shake, shudder...
near the sludgy old swamp.
The dinosaurs are coming.
Get ready to romp.

Donk!

Donk!

Donk!

Here's **Triceratops** jumping UP and DOWN doing dinosaur hops.

He wears three horns
on his **big**, bony head,

and blunders along with a
Bomp! Bomp! tread.

"Shake, shake, shudder"...
near the sludgy old swamp.
The dinosaurs are coming.
Get ready to romp.

Watch out for
Deinosuchus
with her
snip-snap grin,
as she perches
on her tail and
twizzles
in a spin.

Brontosaurus stops for a slushy, mushy snack. His tail starts swinging with a

Thwack! Thwack! Thwack!

"Shake, shake, shudder"... near the sludgy old swamp. The dinosaurs are coming. Get ready to romp.

StegoSaurus stomps along
with lots of her mates.

Clatter! Clatter! Clatter!

go their bony
back plates.

"Shake, shake, shudder"...
near the sludgy old swamp.
The dinosaurs are coming.
Get ready to romp.

Styracosaurus shakes
his collar and his spikes.
Rattle! Rattle! Rattle!
is the noise that he likes!

A pack of **Deinonychuses**
go running by *fast*
with a ZOOM! ZOOM! ZOOM!
so they won't be the last.

"Shake, shake, shudder"...
near the sludgy old swamp.
The dinosaurs are coming.
Get ready to romp.

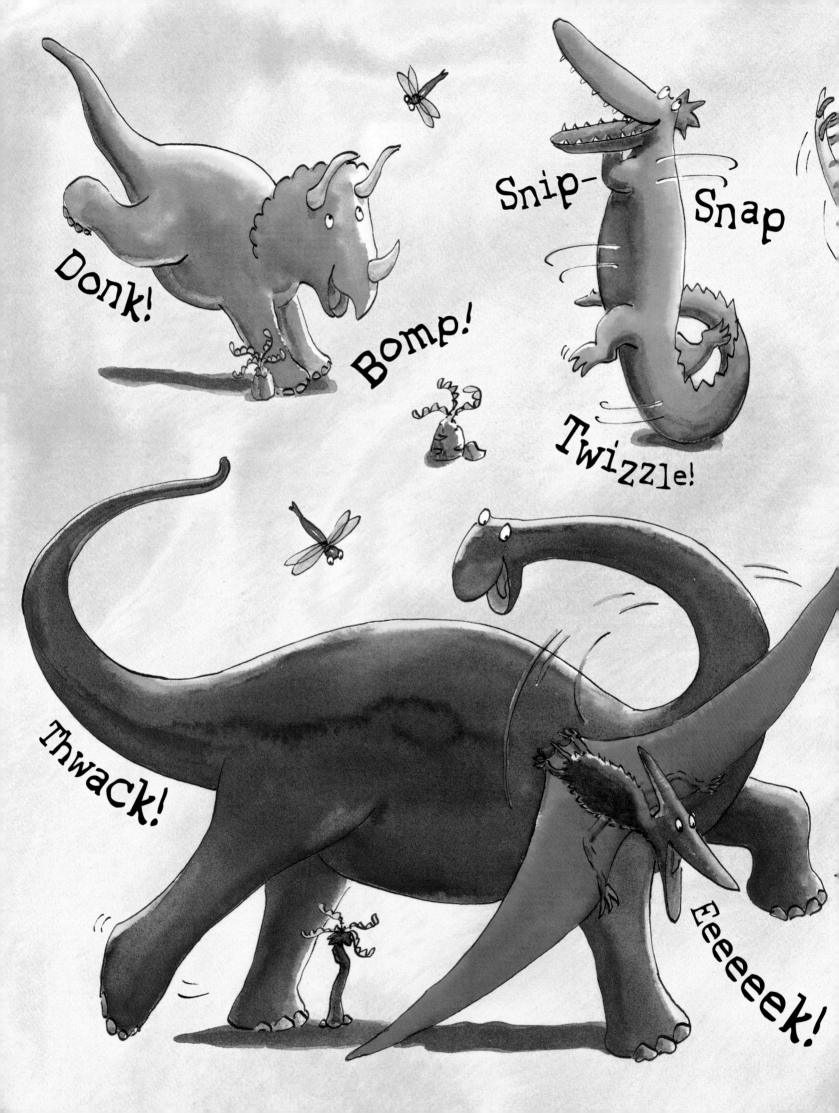

Clatter!

Rattle!

Zoom! Zoom!

Come and take a peek...

"Shake, shake, shudder"...
near the sludgy old swamp.
Everybody's doing the
dinosaur romp.

rrrr...!

Roar! Roar! Roar!
Now we're shivering with fright.
What can make a noise like that
in the night?

Tyrannosaurus crashes in,
gnashing his jaws.

WallOp!

on the ground
go his
big
back
claws.

He's huge
and he's heavy,
but all he wants to do...

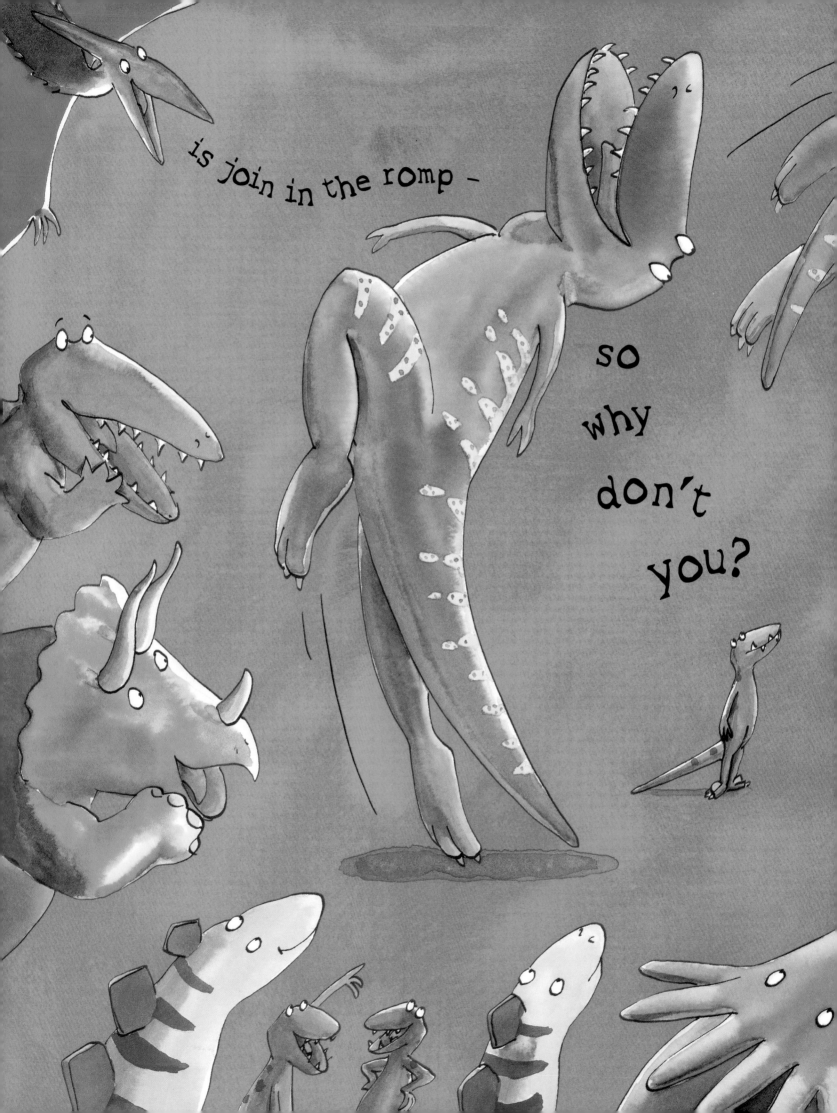

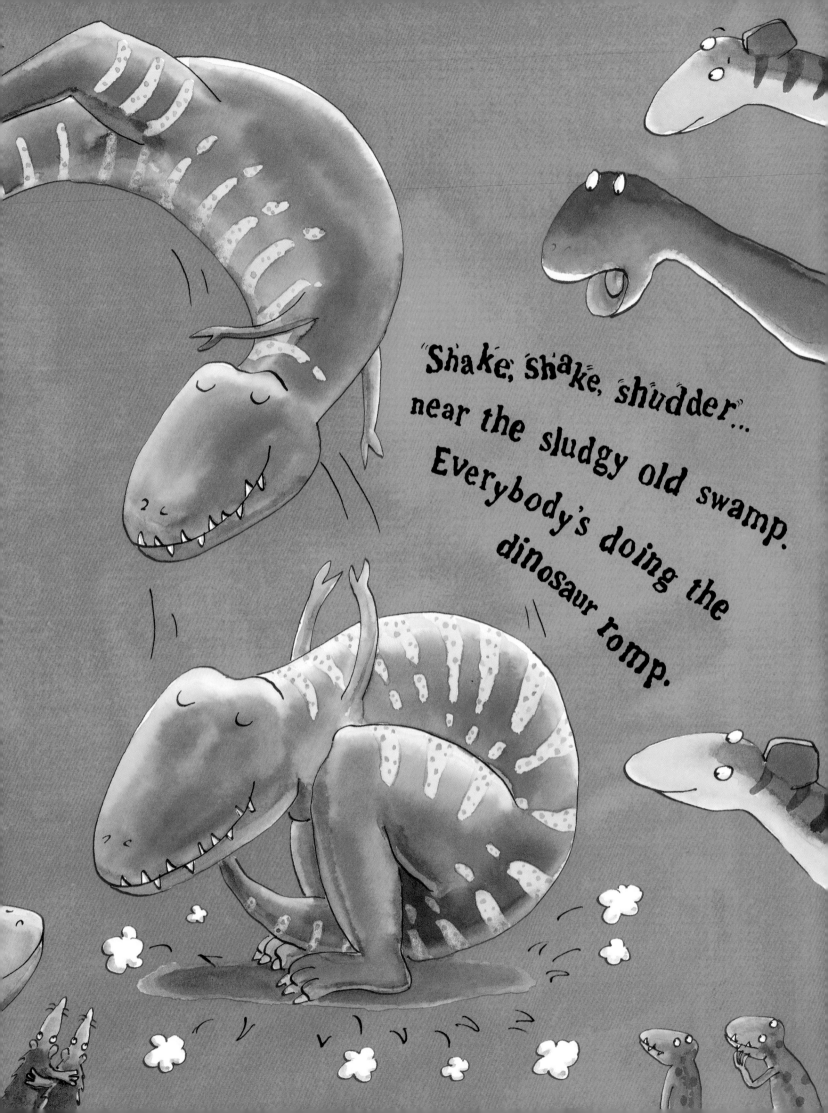

"Shake, shake, shudder...
near the sludgy old swamp.
Everybody's doing the
dinosaur romp.

The dinosaurs won't scratch us,
or bite us, or thump us.
They just want to holler up a...

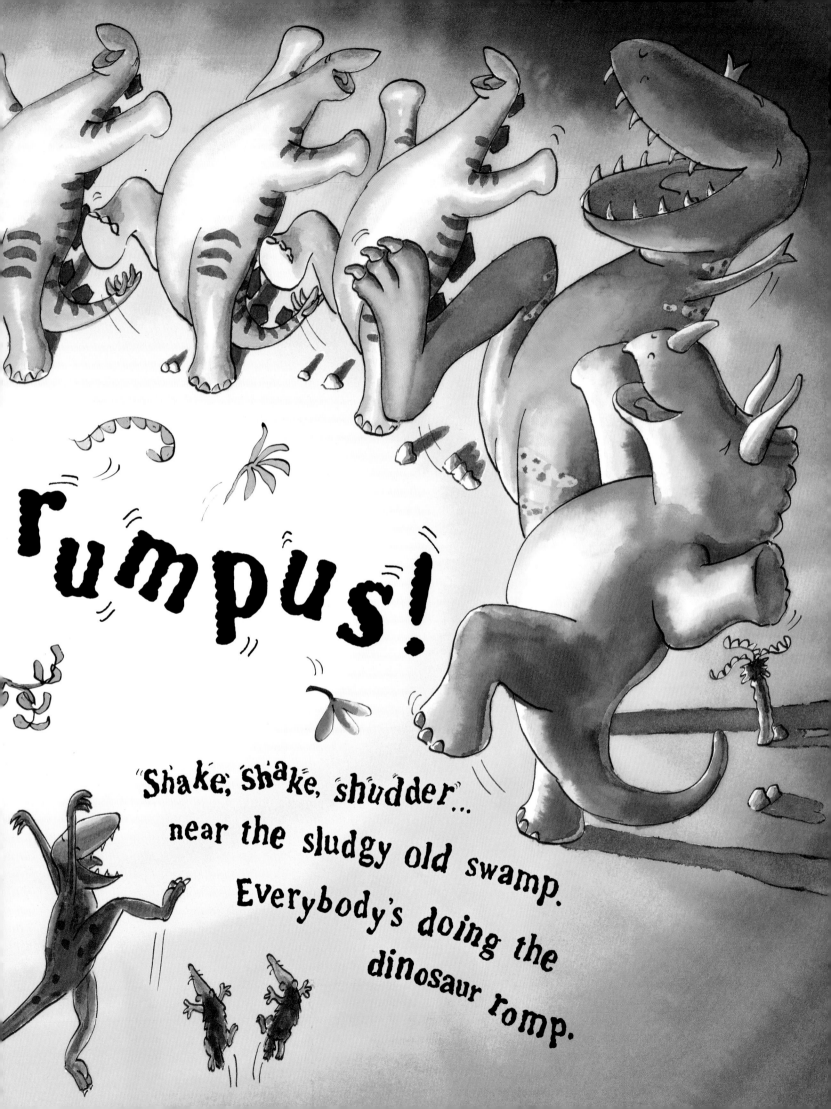

rumpus!

"Shake, shake, shudder...
near the sludgy old swamp.
Everybody's doing the
dinosaur romp.

But soon all the rompers grow sleepy and slow.

The rumpus calms down and the sound drops low.

The rompers drift together
and tumble in a heap...

till finally the dinosaurs
are all fast asleep.

And now the only noise
in the deep of the night
is...

dinosaur-snoring
till the next day's light.